The Brave Beauty Series

Volume 2

Star of Persia

A Story Adapted from the Book of Esther

Marion Dawson Gunderson

Illustrated by Susan Shorter

WestBow
PRESS
A DIVISION OF THOMAS NELSON

Scripture quotations are taken from the NIV
Copyright © 1984

WestBow Press books may be ordered through booksellers or by contacting:

WestBow Press
A Division of Thomas Nelson
1663 Liberty Drive
Bloomington, IN 47403
www.westbowpress.com
1-(866) 928-1240

ISBN: 978-1-4497-6065-6 (sc)
ISBN: 978-1-4497-6066-3 (e)

Library of Congress Control Number: 2012913151

Printed in the United States of America

WestBow Press rev. date: 09/17/2012

For Zoë

Contents

Pronunciations

Esther [ES-ter]
Mordecai [MOR-duh-ky]
Jair [JAY-ur]
Xerxes [ZURK-seez]
Dina [DEE-nah]
Hegai [HEG-eye]
Mei [MAY]
Haman [HAY-mun]
Hathach [HAH-thuk]

1

A New Star

LONG AGO in the ancient kingdom of Persia, a beautiful baby girl was born. Her name was Esther, a word that means *star*. Esther quickly grew into a bright, happy little girl with dark shining eyes. Her hair was glossy chestnut brown streaked with golden highlights from the sun that blazed down upon Persia.

Esther's favorite toy was a little cloth doll with black hair and purple eyes. Her name was Basha, a name that means *daughter of a promise*. Esther took Basha with her everywhere she went.

Esther spent most of her time in the family courtyard, playing with her cousins and her younger brothers, Gabe and Izzy. The children weren't allowed to play in the street where slave traders could kidnap them.

Friday was Esther's favorite day of the week because it was the start of the Sabbath, and she helped with the cooking. She loved doing grown-up jobs.

One Friday, Esther was perched on a stool at the kitchen table, working her fingers through some spongy bread dough. "Is this ready yet, Mama?" she asked.

"Yes Esther, you did a fine job," said Mama with a smile. She lifted the dough from the table, formed it into a plump ball, and plopped it into a wooden bowl. "Now, please set this next to the oven to rise."

Esther jumped down from the stool, slid the heavy bowl off the table, and placed it near the warm clay oven. Then she wiped her hands on her apron, picked up Basha, and sat on the floor. She began braiding tiny ribbons into Basha's hair. "Mama, will we have grapes for the Sabbath?" she asked.

"Yes, purple grapes and Persian melons— and a special surprise for you!" Esther's hands dropped to her lap.

"Pomegranates? Oh, Mama, please say pomegranates!" Esther set Basha in a basket and scrambled onto a stool. She peered anxiously about the kitchen.

Just then, Gabe and Izzy sprang through the doorway. "Papa's home!" shouted Gabe.

"He has gifts!" exclaimed Izzy.

Dashing back to the courtyard, the boys met their father with pleas of, "Please Papa, show us now!" Papa made his way into the house as Izzy leaped and grabbed at his father's shoulder sack shouting, "Let me see! Let *me* see!"

"Calm down, you two!" said Papa, striding toward the kitchen. "Let me greet your mother first."

"Abe!" beamed Mama, "I'm glad you're home early." She hugged her husband, and noticed his bulging shoulder sack. "You must've had a good week at the shop!"

"Indeed!" replied Papa. "Since young Mordecai came to work for us, we've had a lot more time to keep the shelves stocked. You know what we say—"

"Yes, dear, we know what you always say—"

Everyone chimed in, "If you don't *have* it, you can't *sell* it!"

"Now," teased Papa, turning back to the children, "would this be a good time to open my sack?"

"Yes! Open it now!" chorused the boys. Esther watched wide-eyed as her father slung his treasure sack to the floor.

"First, I thought we could add some *music* to our Sabbath," said Papa, handing Gabe and Izzy small wooden flutes with a dancing camel design.

"Thank you, Papa!" said the boys. They began blowing on the flutes while trying to hum a tune. For Esther, there was a child-sized harp adorned with delicate gold tracings.

"Oh thank you, Papa!" cried Esther, "It's beautiful!"

Next, Papa pulled out tiny horses and carts for Gabe and Izzy. The boys shouted in delight, and began racing the toys across the floor.

Grinning at Esther, Papa presented a doll-size table and two tiny chairs. "Papa, they're perfect!" exclaimed Esther. "Thank you." She picked up Basha and sat her on one of the chairs.

"Oh thank you, Papa,"
cried Esther. "It's beautiful!"

"Now here's something for *all* of us," announced Papa, displaying a wooden game board with animal playing pieces.

"I get the lions!" shouted Gabe, grabbing them up.

"Hah! I wanted the bulls anyway!" countered Izzy.

"Boys!" scolded Mama. "Where are your manners?"

"Thank you, Papa," said Gabe.

"Yes, thank you, Papa," said Izzy.

"And now for my lovely wife," said Papa. He presented Mama with a small olivewood jewelry box.

"Abe, what have you been up to?" said Mama, admiring the beautiful design on the box.

"It's from the homeland," said Papa. Esther watched her mother lift the lid.

"Oh my goodness!" gasped Mama. The box held a silver bracelet set with gold flowers. "It's lovely!"

"So are you!" beamed Papa.

"Let me see it Mama!" cried Esther, dancing on tiptoes between her parents. She noticed a

Hebrew inscription etched on the inside of the bracelet. "What does it say?"

"It's from King Solomon's poem," explained Papa. "It says, 'Your beauty shows as a flower among thorns.'"

"Oh, Abe, not *me!*" exclaimed Mama

"Yes, you! You're still my beauty," declared Papa. He ended the little ceremony by sliding the bracelet onto Mama's wrist and kissing her on the cheek.

"Now I think that's everything I brought," said Papa. "Wait! There's something else!" Gabe and Izzy jumped up from their game to see the final surprise. Holding up a net bag bulging with large red fruits Papa said, "For the Sabbath!"

"Pomegranates!" shouted Esther. "This is the best Sabbath ever!"

2

The Blessing

THE AROMA of freshly baked bread filled the house. "Is it time to light the lamps yet?" asked Esther.

"Yes, the sun is at the rooftop," said Mama, glancing across the courtyard. "Please call your brothers in." Esther hurried to the doorway and yelled to Gabe and Izzy. They were having a miniature horse and cart race with some cousins.

Hearing Esther, Papa excused himself from a cluster of men in the courtyard, and collected his sons. "It's almost the Sabbath, you two," said Papa. "Time to wash up."

Mama was waiting at the door. "Please put your toys away," she said.

"Aw, can't we keep them?" whined Gabe. A stern look from Papa sent the boys scurrying to their room. When they returned, Mama steered them to the washbowl with clean towels. Esther set Basha in her basket just inside her bedroom.

While Papa added oil to the lamps, Esther and Mama set out salty green olives, syrupy figs, and five small goblets of pomegranate juice. Some of the pomegranates were served in slices so Gabe and Izzy could have fun plucking out the juicy seeds.

Mama lifted a steaming bowl of lentil stew from the oven and set it at Papa's place. Finally, the fragrant bread arrived on a warm stone platter.

As the children took their places at the table, Mama lit the lamps, signaling the start of the Sabbath. The little room took on a soft glow. Mama sat down next to Papa. Everyone was quiet. Even Izzy's wiggly body was lulled still by the mesmerizing flicker of the lamps. All eyes were on Papa as he stood at the head of the table.

Papa raised his hands heavenward. Mama and the children bowed their heads. "You are the one true God," declared Papa. "We thank you for this day of rest. Our hearts praise you, O God of Israel. Thank you for loving us. Thank you for this family."

Esther thought about her deep love for her family, though Gabe and Izzy could be annoying at times. *God has blessed us,* she thought.

Lowering his hands, Papa finished the prayer. "God, our Maker, we praise you for this food that you have brought forth from the earth. May it make us strong to serve you. Amen."

Now comes my favorite part, thought Esther. *How will Papa bless us this time?*

Papa walked to where Gabe was sitting and placed his hands on the boy's shoulders. "Gabriel, my eldest son," said Papa, "may God give you the courage of Joshua."

Moving to Izzy next, Papa prayed, "Israel, my son, may God give you the obedience of Daniel."

Then, spreading his hands gently on Esther's shoulders, Papa said, "Esther, my sweet daughter, may the God who blessed you with grace and beauty now bless you with—" Papa paused, his eyes closed as he searched for the words. "With the courage of Abigail."

Papa returned to his chair. Mama began the meal by tearing off a piece of the warm bread and offering it to Papa.

Abigail? thought Esther. *Who is Abigail?*

3

The Peacemaker

THE SABBATH morning began in the courtyard with the families gathered to hear the eldest men read the sacred books. Then everyone joined in the singing, with Esther softly strumming her new harp.

At noon, everyone enjoyed an outdoor feast of fresh bread, roasted vegetables, fruit, and stew that had been kept warm in ovens overnight. There were raisin cakes with thick cream for dessert.

As the afternoon sun rose higher, children played in little groups, women chatted under the trees, and men discussed plans for a larger synagogue where they could worship with other Hebrews from the city.

"Mama!" complained Esther, "Gabe's shooting seeds at us again!" Gabe ducked behind a tree, but Mama had already spotted him.

"Gabriel! You come here this instant!" ordered Mama. Gabe appeared from behind the tree and walked slowly toward her, his eyes downcast. Mama stretched out her hand, palm up. Gabe stared at it.

"What?" he asked.

"You know 'what,' Gabriel! Either give me that reed or you will stay inside today." Gabe sighed, shrugged, and sauntered back to the tree. He picked up the hollow reed he'd used to shoot seeds, then sauntered back and placed it in Mama's hand.

"Perhaps God has given you a warrior's heart," said Mama, "but you mustn't use it on your family!"

"Yes, Mama," murmured Gabe. He turned and shot an angry glance at Esther, then disappeared into a group of boys engaged in a toy chariot battle.

"Thank you, Mama," said Esther.

"It won't happen again. Papa will talk to him."

"Gabe kept the seeds from supper," said Esther. "He hid them in his napkin." Esther pointed to a red blotch on her Sabbath gown. "See? One of them left a stain."

"I'm sorry, sweet one," said Mama. "I'll try to clean it tomorrow. We must not work on the Sabbath."

Remembering Papa's blessing, Esther asked, "Mama, who was Abigail?"

"Abigail?"

"From Papa's blessing."

"Oh, yes. That name surprised me too. Papa knows the sacred books so well. Yes, I *do* remember the story of Abigail. She lived at the time of King David. She met David one day, before he was king." Esther followed Mama to a shady bench. "Abigail's husband was a rich man, but he was *very mean.*"

"Why did she marry him?"

"Women usually don't get to choose their husbands."

"Will I get to choose *mine*, Mama? I want a husband just like Papa."

"May God bless you with a good husband, my child. Now, let me finish the story. David helped Abigail's husband a lot, but when David asked for some help in return, Abigail's husband insulted him."

"*Insulted?* What does that mean?"

"It's when you say something—or do something—disrespectful to somebody."

"What was the insult?"

"I can't remember exactly, but in those days, when a man was insulted, it usually ended up in a fight. So David and his men got their swords and were going to kill Abigail's people."

"Including Abigail?" cried Esther, clutching Basha to her chest.

"I don't remember, but they would at *least* have killed the men. So Abigail decided to stop it if she could."

"How could *she* stop it?"

"She was a rich woman, so she decided to give David a big gift. It was her way of fighting evil with good."

"What kind of gift?"

"Food! Lots of it. Abigail and her servants loaded up donkeys with bread, meat, raisin cakes, wine, cheese; the best food they had. Then they went out to meet David and his army."

"She really *was* brave!"

"Yes she was. Now, when Abigail saw David coming with his men, she got off her donkey and bowed so low that her face almost touched the ground. She must have been shaking with fear, but she stood up and told David how sorry she was that her husband had insulted him. Then she showed David the food she'd brought him as a peace offering."

"What did David say?"

"He told Abigail she was a *wise woman!* He thanked her for the food, and promised not to fight with her husband. He praised God for Abigail."

"Wow! So *that's* why Papa blessed me with 'the courage of Abigail.'"

"Yes, precious one. You may not need to save your family some day, but I can promise you there *will* come a time when you'll need courage. It happens to everyone."

"Thanks for telling me about Abigail, Mama." said Esther. She gave her mother a quick hug, then skipped away to join her friends. *Gabe should apologize for shooting seeds at us,* she thought. *It was very insulting!*

4

Royalty

LATER THAT day, as shadows lengthened in the courtyard, families drifted back indoors for afternoon naps and snacking. Gabe and Izzy sat near the doorway, inventing tunes on their flutes. Esther hovered over her new table set, pretending to serve Basha a raisin cake. Mama and Papa chatted quietly in the kitchen.

Suddenly, trumpets sounded in the distance. Mama and Papa stopped talking. Gabe and Izzy halted their music. In the courtyard, women shushed their children. Men fell silent. Only the twittering of birds was heard.

Again the trumpets sounded, closer this time.

"The king!" shouted a child. Other voices echoed the news.

"Papa, can we—"

"No, Gabriel!" warned Papa. "We can't go to the street to watch. It's still the Sabbath."

"But I want to see the horses, Papa!" begged Izzy.

"Papa," asked Esther, in her sweetest voice, "May we watch from *inside* the courtyard?"

"I suppose," said Papa, "but there isn't much room to see." Children were already crowding the front gate.

"Papa?" pleaded Gabe, pointing to a wall where children were being boosted up by their parents.

"Alright, let's go," said Papa, casting a knowing grin to Mama.

"Me first!" yelled Gabe, charging ahead.

Esther skipped along behind, wondering whether she was too old to be lifted by Papa. "Esther!" called a familiar voice. It was Cousin Mordecai striding toward her with a wooden stool. "Here's something to stand on," he said. When they reached the wall, Mordecai steadied the stool and lifted Esther onto it.

Mordecai was Esther's favorite cousin. He was no longer a boy, but a grown man, tall and strong. He worked with Papa and Uncle Jair in the shop. As long as Esther could remember, Cousin Mordecai had always done nice things for people. Basha was a birthday present from him.

"Thank you, Mordecai," said Esther, grabbing a vine to pull herself higher. Standing on her tiptoes, she could see the royal procession approaching. Gabe and Izzy perched on Papa's and Mordecai's shoulders.

The parade was led by heralds, resplendent in red and gold tunics. They blared their silver horns skyward, announcing the approach of the king.

Next came the royal banner bearers, displaying giant tasseled images of Persia's history; its towers and palaces, its two glorious rivers lined with palm groves, its many wild creatures. The largest banner bore the image of Mithras, the king's god, shown as a warrior riding a bull. It cast a shadow across the onlookers as it passed the courtyard.

Izzy and Gabe were dizzy with excitement as the king's soldiers approached on their handsome steeds. Hooves thundered on the pavement. "Look, Papa!" exclaimed Izzy. "Even the *horses* are dressed up!" Indeed, the stallions wore fringed saddlecloths and matching masks. They snorted and whinnied beneath their ornamental headpieces. The warriors held their spears ready and scanned the crowd for any signs of a trouble.

The king rode in a curtained platform called a *litter*. It hung on long poles carried by eight sturdy slaves. Armed guards marched on both sides, their shields glinting in the sun.

Esther could see the litter's purple canopy gently tilting from side to side as the slaves bore the king along. The king was sitting on a throne-like chair. He held a long scepter. A second figure stood next to him.

"Who's that man with the king?" asked Esther.

"That's the prince, the king's oldest son," said Mordecai.

When the litter passed the courtyard, Esther could only see the top of its flower-strewn canopy. As it moved on, she could see its royal occupants. She tapped Mordecai's shoulder. "What's the prince's name?" she asked.

"Xerxes," said Mordecai.

"*Xerxes?* That's a funny name," said Esther. "What does it mean?"

"It means *ruler over heroes.*"

"Cousin Mordecai, you always know *every*thing!"

"I *don't* always know everything!" said Mordecai with a smile, "but I *will* say *this*—it's from the holy books—'Wise men listen and learn.'"

"Does that mean girls too?"

"Of *course* it does!"

They watched as the king and the prince slowly disappeared under the palm trees that lined the road.

Years later..

5

Changes

"ESTHER! WHERE are the new oil lamps? Esther? Are you still here?"

"Yes, Izzy," called Esther from the back room of the shop. "I'm unpacking them right now."

Izzy rearranged the shop's Sabbath display, this time placing the glass goblets next to the gold-rimmed plates from Egypt.

"Here they are!" announced Esther, emerging from the back room carrying two oil lamps. "We have sixteen more in the back. I think they'll look nice with the goblets."

"Let's see," said Izzy, carefully placing them in the display. "Perfect! And Gabe got them at a great price. Just like Papa always said—"

"I remember," said Esther, 'If you don't have it, you can't sell it!'"

Admiring one of the plates, Izzy said, "We never had anything this fancy at home."

"But it didn't matter, did it?" Esther remembered the good family times years ago, when they were children. They still had Mama and Papa then, and spent many hours playing in the courtyard. Sadly, all that had changed when a deadly fever swept through the city, killing many people, including Mama, Papa, and Uncle Jair.

It was customary in those days for an older relative to adopt orphans. Cousin Mordecai hadn't married, so he adopted Esther, Gabe, and Izzy, and became their legal father. Now the four of them lived in a house on the family courtyard.

Gabe and Izzy were now in their teens, and had taken over Mordecai's work at the shop. Mordecai spent his days at the king's palace, where he served as an official for the Hebrew people. Xerxes had succeeded his father, and was now King of Persia.

Esther worked at home, cooking and cleaning for her brothers and Mordecai. She enjoyed chatting with her aunts and cousins as she worked with them in the courtyard. On some days—like this one—she helped Gabe and Izzy in the shop.

Esther had grown into a stunningly beautiful young woman. Although she dressed modestly, men's eyes followed her wherever she went. At the synagogue, young men competed for her attention. In the marketplace, shopkeepers tried not to stare as Esther selected fruit from their bins. Soldiers in the city square were captivated by Esther's graceful beauty. Their eyes followed her as she passed.

In the evenings after dinner, Esther played her harp as the family gathered to chat. On a recent evening, Mordecai said, "You'll never guess what happened today!"

"At the palace?" asked Izzy, looking up from a sign he was making for the shop.

"Yes—at the big party that's been going on there all week."

"All *week*?" exclaimed Esther.

"Wow! They really know how to celebrate up there," said Gabe.

"Here's what happened," said Mordecai. "King Xerxes was in the palace garden entertaining the men. He'd been drinking a

Their eyes followed her as she passed.

lot of wine. His wife, Queen Vashti, was inside the palace entertaining the women. The king decided to show the men how *beautiful* Vashti was, so he sent for her. Well, Queen Vashti didn't like the idea of parading herself in front of all those men, so she refused to go."

"I can't blame her," said Esther.

"Well, that made the king *furious!* He wanted to punish Vashti for embarrassing him in front of the men."

"Did he kill her?" asked Gabe.

"No, he didn't kill her. He didn't know *what* to do, so he asked his advisors. They said he should *banish* Queen Vashti from the palace. They said it would be a good lesson for every wife who disobeys her husband."

"That seems pretty harsh," said Esther.

"Maybe so, but that's exactly what he did. This morning, he sent out a royal decree to every province in the kingdom. It says Vashti is no longer queen. It says she is banished from the palace. It also says husbands should rule over their wives."

"Where is she now?" asked Izzy.

"I don't know," said Mordecai, "but she's gone."

Everyone was silent for a moment, reflecting on the news. Finally, Esther said, "It's sad. Maybe he really loved her. Maybe he'll *miss* her. Mordecai, do you think he was too harsh?"

"Perhaps. He was certainly too *pride*ful. Sometimes people drink too much, and then do things they regret later. Lesson learned, right?"

"Right," they all agreed.

6

Shadows

A FEW DAYS later, Esther was helping Izzy in the shop while Gabe was out getting more things to sell. She finished unpacking the crates, dusted everything in the shop, and then artfully placed new merchandize on display shelves.

After sharing a lunch of cheese and fruit with Izzy, Esther headed for the market to buy some things for supper. She was a few steps beyond the shop when she heard familiar voice.

"Esther!"

"Gabe?" She turned to see her brother's lanky frame rushing toward her. He was soaked with sweat and wearing a pained expression.

"Gabe, what is it?" cried Esther. "What's happened?"

Gasping for breath, Gabe sputtered, "No time to explain. Just cover your face and get home!"

"But we need some things for the Sabbath!" objected Esther. Gabe fumbled to pull his sister's shoulder scarf over her face.

"What do we need?" asked Gabe. "I'll get it." His voice carried an authority Esther had never heard before.

"Um, let's see," said Esther. "We need a jug of olive oil, some grapes—purples ones—and four pigeon eggs."

"Olive oil, grapes, and four eggs. Got it. Now get home! This is *serious*, Esther. I'll explain later."

"But, Gabe, what's this all about? Just tell me *some*thing!"

"Alright," said Gabe. Drawing close to Esther, he said, "This is the problem, my sister: You're too pretty. Now *go!*" He turned and headed for the market.

Esther walked quickly toward home. As she tightened her scarf about her face, she noticed her hands trembling. A chill passed through her. She was gripped with a foreboding, as if something terrible was about to happen.

"Too pretty?" She whispered to herself. "Too *pretty? How can *that* be a problem?"

As she entered the courtyard, Esther slowed her pace, then froze in midstep. Something was wrong. There were no children playing; no women working outside. The courtyard was deserted except for a group of men—all uncles and cousins—gathered under a shade tree. Their voices were hushed, their faces serious. Mordecai was there. He noticed Esther, and motioned for her to go into the house.

Mordecai home in the middle of the day? thought Esther. *What could it be?* She entered the coolness of the kitchen, unwound her scarf, and hung it by the stove to dry.

Trying to shrug off the dread that was starting to paralyze her, Esther set about preparing supper. *First the bread; that takes the longest.* She measured out the flour and set the yeast in water. *What could be happening? Has someone brought shame on us? Is it me? Did I do something wrong?* Esther tried to stifle her fears by furiously chopping the vegetables.

Just then, Mordecai entered. Instead of his usual cheery greeting, he walked solemnly to his favorite chair and slumped into it. Esther rushed to him and knelt. "Oh Mordecai! Tell me what's happening! First Gabe sent me home, and now you and the men are talking. What *is* it? Did I do something wrong?"

"No, daughter," said Mordecai with a smile. "You've done nothing wrong. It's something *Xerxes* is doing."

"Xerxes? I thought he liked our people."

"It isn't just us; it's *every*body. You see, King Xerxes has decided he wants a new queen—someone to replace Vashti."

"Why is *that* a problem?"

"It *could* be a problem for us because of the *way* he's going about it. Instead of choosing a queen from the women he knows, he's issued a royal decree calling for the most beautiful maidens of the *entire kingdom* to be brought to him. He'll choose one of them."

"I still don't see why that should concern us," said Esther.

"The women will be *ordered* to go to this 'beauty contest.' That's what they're calling it. The women won't have a choice about it. That's how the king gets most of his soldiers. He just *takes* them."

"I see," said Esther, pulling up a chair next to Mordecai. They sat quietly, pondering what it could mean for them.

"That's why Gabe sent me home," reflected Esther. "He thinks I'm pretty."

"Yes, you *are* beautiful, Esther. Gabe must have seen the decree. He was protecting you."

"There are *lots* of girls who would *love* to be queen," said Esther, "but not me! I want a good Hebrew husband like Papa, not some *Mithras* worshipper who doesn't know God—even if he *is* king!"

"I know, my child," said Mordecai, patting Esther's hand. "I want that for you too. Just to be safe, you will stay home until this is over. Our young women will stay inside. Gabe and Izzy will do the shopping for you, and one of them will stay here with you all the time."

"You don't think the king's men will come *here*, do you?"

"We don't know. For now we'll take this precaution, and leave the rest to God."

Later, Mordecai stood at the Sabbath table. The oil lamps cast shadows of his tall figure onto the walls. The aroma of the warm bread did little to calm the fears gripping the little family. They sat with their heads bowed, waiting for Mordecai's words. *Will this be our last Sabbath together?* thought Esther. *Lord, let it not be!*

Raising his hands in praise, Mordecai declared, "You are the one true God! Thank you for this Sabbath. Thank you for this home and this family you've given me; Gabriel, so strong and faithful. Israel, a joyful servant." And then, with a tremor in his voice, he said, "And Esther, my sweet daughter, full of love and grace." He paused. Izzy squeezed back tears.

How could I live without my family? thought Esther.

"Lord, calm our hearts," continued Mordecai. "We claim the promise you gave us through your prophet Isaiah: 'Do not fear, for I am with you. I will strengthen you and help you.' Thank you for this food, and for the loving hands that prepared it. Amen."

Mordecai sat down and cleared his throat. Esther tore off a piece of the loaf and offered it to him. The meal continued in silence for a moment or two, everyone lost in thought.

Finally Esther spoke. "Thank you for buying the groceries, Gabe."

"No problem! I enjoy the market. Shopping is one of my many talents, you know."

"Not so fast!" countered Esther. "Soon Xerxes' 'beauty contest' will be over and *I'll* be the shopper again!"

"I'm sorry," said Izzy, eyeing the empty shelf. "We just sold the last one this morning. The lion and bull game is a popular item."

"I know," said the customer, an elderly man with a kind face. "I had one when I was a boy, and now my grandson wants one."

"We played it years ago," said Izzy. "My father brought it home from this shop. My brother usually keeps them in stock, but he's been at home with my sister this week."

"I see. Well, for now I'll take some of those new glass balls the boys are wanting these days."

"We have large and small ones," offered Izzy.

"I'll take some of both."

Izzy reached into a bin and scooped up two handfuls of marbles. "How's this?" he asked.

"Fine! I'll take them." Izzy dropped the marbles into a small pouch and tied it with a string. The customer paid and left the shop promising, "I'll be back when you get more board games."

"Sure!" called Izzy. "When they come in, I'll display one in the window. See you then."

Whew! thought Izzy. *We're running out of stock. I wish Xerxes would pick a new queen so Gabe can come back to work.*

Izzy grabbed a broom and began sweeping. Suddenly, Cousin Jacob burst through the doorway. "Israel!" cried, "They've taken Esther! You'd better come!"

"No!" shouted Izzy, dropping the broom.

Gabe sat at the table, his head tilted back while two aunts dabbed sesame oil on the angry welts rising on his face. Izzy stood over him in shock, hoping it was a bad dream.

"I told them Esther is the only woman in our family," said Gabe, wincing as salty tears collected in an open cut. "I told them our father worked at the palace. It didn't matter to them."

"Who were they?" asked Izzy.

"A palace official and two guards. I recognized one of the guards from the market. I tried blocking the door, but they knocked me down and beat me."

"Did they hurt Esther?"

"No. She screamed at them when they hit me. She begged me to stop fighting back. She shouted, 'Gabriel! Let *God* do the fighting for us!'"

7

The Maidens

ESTHER SAT sobbing on a velvet cushion inside the royal litter. Tears rolled down her cheeks and splashed onto her hands, which were tied with a cord. Her head throbbed from the horror of being dragged from her home. Her stomach churned from the swaying of the litter as the king's slaves carried it toward the palace.

Heavy curtains blocked out the light. Esther's head was draped in a purple veil embroidered with the king's symbol, a panther. She was vaguely aware of someone else in the litter.

"Esther?" said a nearby voice.

"Y-yes?" answered Esther.

"This is Dina."

"Dina? From the synagogue?"

"Yes. I thought I recognized your voice when they put you in here."

"Are we the only ones here?" asked Esther

"Yes."

"Dina! I'm so sorry you've been taken!"

"I'm sorry for you, too, Esther."

"Did you tell them you were engaged to be married?"

"Yes, but it didn't matter to them."

"They have no respect for our people!" declared Esther.

"They have no respect for *any*one!" cried Dina. "They're rounding up every girl who looks good to the soldiers. Oh, Esther, our lives are *over!*" Dina dissolved into sobs.

"Don't give up, Dina! Remember God's promise: 'I will never leave you or forsake you.'"

"But I *feel* forsaken!" cried Dina.

"I do too, but we can't trust our feelings. We have to trust His promises. Remember Joseph, the Hebrew who was taken to Egypt as a slave?"

"Yes, a little, but what does that have to do with us? He was a *boy!*"

"True, but—" Suddenly the litter stopped. A gruff voice barked through the silk curtains, "Quiet in there! We're at the palace!"

Step by step, the litter was lifted up the giant stone steps to the palace gate. Esther pictured the towering lion statues on either side. She had seen them many times. She remembered the enormous wooden doors, with their carved images of Persian soldiers.

Mordecai was usually at the gate. He often posted himself there so Hebrews could bring their problems to him.

Dina slid closer to Esther and whispered, "Isn't your father at the gate?"

"Usually," whispered Esther, "but he warned me to keep my family a secret if I were ever captured."

"*Why?*"

"Our people have enemies everywhere."

The litter came to a stop. The guards sent for someone named Hegai, a name that means *separation*. Esther wondered if Mordecai was nearby. *Does he even know I've been taken?* she thought. She was tempted to cry out, but she remembered his warning.

Soon heavy footsteps approached. The drapes were yanked aside. Sunlight flooded the compartment. "Yes, they wear the king's veil," said a male voice. "Take them to the maidens' quarters."

The two captives were pulled from the litter, their hands still tied in front of them. The gigantic wooden doors creaked open. Rough hands gripped the frightened girls and pushed them through the gate.

The pavement shook as the giant doors slammed shut. Esther and Dina were taken across a vast courtyard that surrounded the palace. Esther could see the pavement passing beneath her feet. It was made of brightly colored tiles set in a swirly pattern.

The maidens were pushed through a doorway into a small room. They were ordered to sit on a cold marble bench. Minutes passed. It was quiet except for the shuffling of the guards' feet, and the occasional clanking of their swords.

Esther could hear the *whoosh, whoosh* of blood pulsing through her ears. She steadied herself with Mordecai's words from Isaiah: "Do not fear, for I am with you. I will—"

A door swung open. Hegai, the king's official in charge of maidens, entered with two woman servants. His stout body was clothed in yards of billowy black silk accented with ropes of gold jewelry. His fat fingers sparkled with large gems. His pudgy face was topped by a stiff black hat set with a large ruby in front. Velvet slippers clad his chubby feet.

"Stand!" ordered Hegai. Esther and Dina rose to their feet. Esther drew her shoulders back, bracing for whatever would come. "Let's see the taller one," commanded Hegai. A servant lifted Esther's veil and draped it about her shoulders. "Hmm," said Hegai, his bulging gray eyes studying Esther's beautiful face and figure.

"Exquisite—the best we've seen," concluded Hegai. Esther felt degraded, as if she were a chicken hanging in the market. "Tell me your name," demanded Hegai.

Lord, give me strength! prayed Esther. "Sir, my name is Esther." She spoke in Aryan, to conceal her Hebrew background.

"And where do you come from, Esther?"

"I live here in the city," she heard herself say.

"You live here in the *palace* now!" snapped Hegai. "I see you speak the king's tongue. Do you speak other languages?"

"Sir, I speak a little Egyptian and Hindi—and some Hebrew." Esther was amazed at how calm she felt.

"And how have you come by such learning, Esther?"

"I come from a family of merchants, sir. My father taught me the languages he uses in his trade."

"I see," said Hegai.

Turning to Dina, Hegai ordered her veil removed. Dina was shaking with fear. Her face was wet with tears. "And who have we here?" said Hegai.

Dina stared at the floor.

"Let me see your face!" demanded Hegai.

Following Esther's lead, Dina spoke in Aryan. "My n-name is—"

Hegai grabbed Dina's chin and jerked it up. "Look at me, miss!" he roared. "Now tell me your name!"

"Oh, please, sir!" pleaded Dina. "Please let me go! I am engaged to be married!"

"You are a servant of the *king!*" roared Hegai, his pudgy hand tightening on Dina's jaw. "Now say your name!"

Dina closed her eyes and whimpered, "I—am Dina." She fought to keep her knees from buckling.

Hegai stepped back and circled the bench slowly, studying the two maidens from every angle. *Lord, calm our hearts!* Esther prayed.

Hegai gave orders to his servants. "Untie them and give them the usual treatments—for now."

Esther and Dina were escorted to another room where they stood waiting. Dina was sobbing. Esther hugged her and dabbed her tears with her scarf.

Soon a woman entered and stood before them. She was beautiful. She was not young, but she had obviously seen the best of care. Her skin was radiant and smooth, not wrinkled like most women her age.

A sapphire blue gown draped the woman's slender figure. Gold cords held it in place. Her bluish purple eyes were traced with dark liner.

Her lips were painted a rich red. An abundance of highlighted chestnut hair was drawn into a jeweled clasp at the crown of her head. The scent of jasmine surrounded her. "Welcome to the king's service," she began with a pleasant smile. "I am Artemis. You have been brought here to possibly become the next queen of Persia."

Artemis paused for a moment to inspect the girls closely. She continued, "My job is to see that you are made suitable for the king. You will be bathed, given beauty treatments, and trained to behave properly in the presence of royalty. You will be dressed in the finest gowns and presented to Xerxes, King of Persia. Do you understand?"

Esther and Dina stared in stunned silence.

"Are there any questions?" asked Artemis.

"Yes, ma'am," ventured Esther.

"You may address me as Artemis."

"Yes, Artemis. I'm wondering how long it will take to do all that you describe?"

"It takes *many months* to make an ordinary woman pleasing to the king," explained Artemis. A little gasp escaped from Dina.

"But what about our *families?*" objected Esther.

"You *have* no families!" declared Artemis. "Nor do I. You see, I am a slave also." A hint of emotion entered her voice. "*Forget* your families. Your lives are *within these walls!* Now, I will escort you to your quarters."

Artemis led Esther and Dina through a short hallway that opened into the largest room Esther had ever seen. Its tall ceiling was supported by columns of pink marble. The walls were draped with rich tapestries depicting scenes of lush forests, exotic flowers, and graceful animals. Statues of beautiful women in Persian gowns graced the entrances.

The scent of sandalwood mingled with the voices of young women seated in the middle of the room. They chatted on plush satin couches. The fragrant air was kept in motion by slave girls waving fans made of peacock feathers.

Pausing on the gleaming floor, Artemis explained, "This is our hair styling parlor." Motioning toward the window area, she added, "We have twenty stylists." Esther could see the silhouettes of hairdressers at work behind curtains.

As Artemis led the captives across the room, the seated maidens grew quiet and studied the newcomers. Esther glanced their way and smiled. She noticed some had bronze skin like hers. Others had dark, satiny skin. Two had light skin and honey colored hair. They were all beautiful.

Esther turned to Artemis and whispered, "Where are these maidens from?"

"The kingdom includes all the lands from India to Africa. Maidens are being brought here from every province."

"How many provinces are there?" asked Esther.

"One hundred twenty-seven."

"I see," said Esther. *That means hundreds of maidens competing!* she thought. *Not much chance of winning.* She smiled at the prospect of being rejected and sent home.

Artemis led Esther and Dina to a covered walkway that opened to the courtyard on one side. The closed side had a series of arched doorways opening to a cosmetic studio, a skin care parlor, a bathing area, a dressing room, and a jewelry vault.

As they neared the end of the colonnade, the aroma of food came wafting out of an entryway. "After you are bathed and dressed, you will dine here," explained Artemis. "Please wait to be called. Now let me show you your sleeping quarters."

They entered a large, fragrant room spread with sleeping mats. Each mat was enclosed by sheer curtains. The silk mats were filled with soft feathers. A few maidens rested on their mats. Others sat together, chatting quietly.

Esther remembered her sleeping mat at home. She pictured its soft cover with her girlhood doll, Basha, propped on the pillow. A pang of homesickness swept over her. She comforted herself by softly patting Dina on the shoulder.

"This sleeping chamber is for newly arrived maidens," explained Artemis. "If you do well, your surroundings will improve." With that, she gave instructions to two of the servants and left.

The servants led Esther and Dina to the bath area where they were assigned separate pink marble tubs filled with warm, perfumed water. They were shown how to shave their arms and legs using curved metal blades and oil. Dina refused to pick up the shaving tool. She stood weeping and shivering near her tub. Finally, she lowered herself into the water to get warm.

Esther decided that shaving would not break Hebrew law, so she sank into the water and began scraping her legs. The warm water relaxed the two women. Dina stopped crying.

After their baths, the maidens donned soft robes and were taken to the beauty parlor. Esther's hair was dried and given a simple brushing until it hung softly about her shoulders. "You have beautiful hair, miss," said the hairdresser.

"Thank you," said Esther. *Papa said my beauty was a blessing,* thought Esther, *but it doesn't seem so now!* Then, refusing to give in to despair, she vowed, *God is in control!*

In the dressing room, Esther chose a pale blue gown tied at the waist with a silver cord. It complimented her bronze skin. Silver hoop earrings and slippers completed her outfit.

Dina showed no preference for any of the gowns, so the attendant dressed her in pale yellow accented by a flowing scarf attached at one shoulder.

8

A Banquet

As Esther and Dina entered the banquet hall, the aroma of roast meat and fresh bread reminded Esther of home, but the heavy fragrance of cedar and myrrh told her she was dining at the king's palace.

The hall was alive with the chatter of maidens, the clatter of dishes, and the tunes of court musicians strolling among the diners. Servants glided about with trays of steaming food.

Esther and Dina were led to a low dining table where they sat on velvet cushions. It was reserved for the maidens who had arrived that day. Some of the new arrivals were already seated and engaged in conversation. Some spoke in Aryan about their homes and families, the trip to the palace, and their new surroundings. Two Indian maidens chatted in Hindi.

"I'm so excited!" exclaimed one girl. "I've always dreamed of living in a palace. The clothes, the jewelry, the—"

"What about the king?" asked another. "Is he old? Is he handsome? I've never seen him."

"I've heard he's *young* and handsome!" exclaimed the first girl. "I can't wait to meet him!"

"You will meet him when you are ready, my dear!" declared Artemis, arriving at the table. She wore a deep pink gown adorned with shimmering beads. The maidens halted their chatter.

"Listen carefully," began Artemis, surveying the maidens. "A queen will not please the king if she does not listen carefully."

Artemis stepped to the head of the table and stood by the cushion. "You notice I am last to be seated. That is because I am *highest in rank* here. The highest-ranking person is always seated last. Do you understand?" Some of the maidens nodded "yes," but others seemed confused. Esther leaned toward the two Indian women and whispered to them in Hindi, after which they nodded to Artemis.

"Good!" said Artemis. "Now pay attention. You do not *flop* down on your cushion nor *step* on your cushion. Watch closely while I demonstrate. You keep your feet to the *side* of your cushion and lower yourself, like this." Artemis alit on the cushion as gently as a butterfly. "Let your gown drape across your slippers. Do not let your ankles show! Understand?" Everyone nodded.

"Now for the feast!" announced Artemis, giving a quick double clap. Male servants appeared instantly, balancing large trays of food.

"Do not look at the servers!" cautioned Artemis. "The king may think you are flirting with them. Just point to your selections and you will be served. Choose what you wish, but remember, women of nobility do not *stuff* themselves!"

Artemis was served first. The maidens watched closely as she chose a small portion of fish topped with peach sauce, a green salad with goat cheese, and fruit in almond sauce. Another servant offered her a choice of wines and juices in elaborate stemmed goblets. Artemis chose a golden wine. She waved off the servants without a word.

The selections were offered to the maidens. *I hope some of this food is allowed!* thought Esther, remembering the strict Hebrew laws that governed her meals. Dina was thinking the same thing. They exchanged knowing glances.

"I believe you will each find something to satisfy your taste," said Artemis. "We serve delicacies from every region of the empire." Esther chose a small portion of roast lamb and rice served with a brown sauce and a salad sprinkled with pistachio nuts. Dina chose lamb and rice too, but skipped the salad in favor of eggplant and green beans. Both took a goblet of pomegranate juice.

Esther bowed her head and quietly thanked God for the food. She asked Him for strength and wisdom.

During dinner, Artemis instructed the women on how a queen should behave at the table. She paused after each rule so that Esther could repeat it in different languages.

"First," began Artemis, "do not *gulp* your food. Eat *slowly*. Chew with your mouth *closed*."

The maidens watched as Artemis patted her lips with her napkin. "Do not leave food on your face.

"Smile," she continued. "Engage in *pleasant* conversation. Always agree with the king. *Never* argue or offer your opinion. Don't chatter too much or wave your hands about.

"Don't criticize! You never know who might be offended.

"*Never* boast about anything but the *king*.

"Do not giggle constantly.

"Do not get drunk on wine.

"Never weep at the table.

"*Never* speak of your family. *No*body here *cares* about your family or your past!

"Do not speak to the servants unless you ask for something." On and on she went about how the queen should behave. By the end of the meal, Esther was feeling that a "proper" queen was a silent, brainless *ornament*.

When dessert came, Dina had eaten just two bites of her meal. Her lamb and rice sat cold on her plate. "Dina!" whispered Esther. "You must eat! We need to stay *strong!*"

"Strong for what?" said Dina. "To be a slave of the king?"

"We don't *know* why God has us here," said Esther.

"I'm just not hungry," sighed Dina. "I feel sick."

The meal concluded with a selection of dainty cakes shaped like flowers and topped with berries and cream. "Here, try this," urged Esther, placing one on Dina's dessert plate.

"Enjoying the banquet, ladies?" Esther turned to see Hegai's toadlike eyes surveying the maidens. "You all look lovely this evening," he said. "I trust you are finding the feast and the music to your satisfaction?"

Some of the women nodded shyly. "You are welcome to linger here in the banquet hall to enjoy the entertainment," said Hegai. "Tonight we are featuring dancers, jugglers, and a sword swallower. You are *also* free to relax in the courtyard. Tomorrow you will begin your beauty treatments."

With that, Hegai motioned to Artemis. She excused herself from the table with a last bit of advice. "Enjoy the entertainment ladies, but remember, a queen never dances in public. It isn't dignified!"

Esther and Dina wanted to escape the incense laden air of the banquet hall, so they made their way outside. The courtyard was paved with tiny glazed tiles arranged to depict Persian birds and flowers. At the center was a reflecting pool dotted with pink and white water lilies.

The courtyard was enclosed by a brick wall built in an open weave pattern that allowed breezes to waft through. The evening air was fragrant with the scent of jasmine from the vines that spilled over the wall. The sun had dipped below the palace roof, leaving the sky a soft orange.

Some of the maidens strolled in small groups, chatting about their new life. Others stared quietly into the reflecting pool. Esther and Dina settled onto a bench under an almond tree near the wall.

"Are you feeling any better, Dina?" asked Esther.

"Yes, I think the fresh air is helping."

"Good. Just take some deep breaths and relax."

"Relax? How can I relax when I don't know what's happening from one minute to the next?"

"Neither did Joseph," said Esther.

"Joseph?"

"The one I mentioned when we were in the litter today. I keep thinking about him."

"Oh yes. The one who was a slave in Egypt."

"Yes. He was from our homeland, but his brothers sold him to slave traders."

"Why?"

"They were jealous of him because their father treated him better than the others. He let Joseph laze around while the others had to work."

"Oh." Dina suddenly felt homesick for her family.

"Anyway," continued Esther, "when Joseph was taken to Egypt, all kinds of bad things happened to him. But he honored God anyway."

"So how did it end?"

"In the end, he was a ruler over Egypt—second only to Pharaoh. They call their kings *pharaohs.*"

"I don't want to be ruler over anything. I just want to go home!" cried Dina.

"Me too," said Esther.

"Then what does this story have to do with us?"

"We need to be like Joseph and do our best, no matter what."

"What do you mean 'do our best?' I don't *want* to be queen of Persia, do you?"

"No, I don't; I want to go home too," said Esther, "but we need to have a good attitude. We need to be excellent—and trust God."

"Did Joseph ever see his brothers again?"

"Oh yes. They were so sorry for what they'd done to him that Joseph forgave them—*and* he saved them from starvation."

"Starvation?"

"Yes. Our people had run out of food up in Canaan, and Joseph had lots of it in Egypt. The point is, what they did to Joseph was evil, but God made something *good* come from it. Maybe something good will come from this evil that's happening to us."

"I just hope *our* families end up together again," said Dina.

Just then, Artemis and Hegai entered the courtyard and settled onto a bench. They were obviously discussing the maidens. At one point, they talked at length while looking toward Esther and Dina.

This made the two friends uncomfortable, so they rose and began strolling toward the reflecting pool. Suddenly Dina whispered, "Esther!"

"What?"

"Esther, I just saw someone outside the wall."

"Who?" said Esther, scanning the wall.

"Don't look over there," cautioned Dina. "Just keep walking."

"Is it someone you know, Dina?"

"Well, I just caught a glimpse of him, but I'm almost certain it was your *father!*"

Esther's heart leaped. *Mordecai! Yes, it must be Mordecai! He's allowed inside the gates.*

"Dina," whispered Esther. "It *could* be my father. Let's walk back along the wall so Artemis and Hegai can't see our faces."

The two women turned and strolled near the wall, their eyes scanning the openings in the brickwork. Suddenly a shadowy form appeared among the jasmine vines. Then a face. It was Mordecai!

9

479 B.C.

*E*STHER AWOKE to the chirping of birds outside her bedchamber. For a moment, she felt like she was back in her girlhood home, waking to the sounds of the courtyard. She remembered Mama and Papa's hushed voices as they moved about the house, trying not to wake the children.

"Your bath is ready, miss!" The maid's voice jarred Esther back to her new surroundings, a luxurious apartment in the palace. She'd been moved there by Hegai, who thought she was an outstanding candidate for queen. She'd been set apart to receive special beauty treatments.

"Thank you! I'll be right there!" called Esther. She drew back the curtains that enclosed her tall feather bed. She had spent many mornings soaking in perfumed baths and having her skin scrubbed with powdered ostrich shells.

Facials of honey and hippo fat had made her skin radiant. Her hair was soft and shiny from soaking in precious oil of myrrh. *Ugh!* thought Esther. *Another day of treatments.* She was bored with the routine, but made the best of it by befriending the servants assigned to her.

Esther didn't like the idea of having servants, but Hegai had given her seven. Fortunately, four of them spoke foreign tongues, so Esther began learning the new languages. Some of the servants were captives like Esther, but others were free to leave the palace and go home to their families at night.

In the evenings, Esther visited the other maidens, comforting those who were scared or homesick. She wove ribbons into their hair while telling them about the real God. Many of them had worshipped gods made of wood or stone. Esther soothed the maidens to sleep with soft music from a wonderful new harp Hegai had given her.

Dina was no longer there. She'd become weak and developed a deep, wheezing cough.

She'd been sent home. *Why couldn't I have gotten sick?* thought Esther in a moment of despair. She knew the answer. *God has a different plan for me.*

Now, as Esther slipped from between the silky sheets, she thought of her favorite part of the day—a message or visit from Mordecai. Would he whisper to her through the jasmine vines along the wall or would she find a note delivered by one of her servants? Perhaps there would be news of Dina.

"Esther, are you up?" called a voice from the hallway.

"Yes, Artemis. Come in!"

"This will just take a moment," said Artemis, stepping into the morning light that filled the bedchamber. She quietly closed the door behind her and looked steadily at Esther, who was perched on the side of her bed.

"After all these months of treatments," began Artemis, "you will be doing something *different* today. We'll start your final preparations before meeting the king." The word *final* had a chilling effect on Esther. She had never given up hope that *something* would save her from standing before the king. That hope was fading.

"After you've dressed and had your breakfast," said Artemis, "you will report to the wardrobe salon to select a gown from our best collection. Then you will go to the cosmetic studio for your make-up. We'll also visit the jewelry vault. This will be a welcome change from your routine, don't you think?"

"Yes, it sounds—exciting, Artemis," answered Esther, trying to force some enthusiasm into her voice.

"See you then!" Artemis turned and left, closing the door behind her. Esther sat motionless, staring at the closed door and wondering whether a door was closing on the life she had always wanted. A life with Mordecai, Gabe, and Izzy. A life full of aunts and uncles and cousins. A life with a good Hebrew husband.

"Now hold perfectly still and don't blink." The cosmetic artist's brush held dark powder mixed in olive oil. She painted a fine line around Esther's eyes. "People will notice your eyes and not know why. There. Perfect! Now for a little color."

The artist brushed Esther's eyelids with shimmering blue-green powder ground from pearly shells. Next, she held a tiny jar of reddish orange powder ground from the anthers of crocus blossoms. She applied it to Esther's cheeks. Last came matching lipstick.

"That's a perfect shade for your gown," said the artist. She applied glistening oil to Esther's lips. "Stunning! The king won't be able to take his eyes off you."

Esther studied herself in the mirror. Her eyes seemed larger. Her skin glowed like the sky at sunrise. She glanced at the silk gown draped across a nearby sofa. "Yes," agreed Esther, "It will be perfect with my gown. Thank you."

"What color is this gown, miss?" asked the artist, running her hand over the luxurious fabric. "It's unusual."

"It's a shade of *amber*," explained Esther, holding the deep orange gown against her body.

"It looks good on you."

"Thank you," said Esther. "Amber means *God is present*. I know God will be with me when I wear it for the king."

The two women stood inside the jewelry vault. A guard hovered nearby, watching their every move. Esther wore a bib-shaped necklace set with dozens of fiery opals.

"What do you think?" asked Artemis.

"It's lovely," said Esther, studying her reflection.

"And here are the earrings." Artemis held up two sparkling cascades of matching opals.

"How exquisite!" exclaimed Esther.

"Now for a bracelet."

"But I prefer to wear *this* bracelet," said Esther, extending her wrist. Artemis inspected the silver and gold bracelet. "It was a gift from my father to my mother."

"Your little bracelet is lovely, dear," said Artemis, "but you really need something that says *royalty*."

"But see how it goes with the set?" Esther held it next to the necklace.

"Not really. It's too ordinary," said Artemis.

"But I *always* wear this bracelet!" insisted Esther. "I never take it off."

"Alright," said Artemis. She handed Esther an opal bracelet that matched the set. "You may wear them *both*."

"Oh, thank you, Artemis!"

"Now," said Artemis, carefully placing the jewelry back in the vault, "tomorrow you will dress completely—gown, hair, make-up, jewelry—everything."

"Will I be taken to the king?" asked Esther, as a shiver of fear passed through her.

"Not yet. Hegai must approve your outfit and give you some instructions. We'll visit the perfumery in the morning, and see Hegai in the afternoon. For now, you need to run along to your apartment and get some rest so your eyes will be bright tomorrow."

Arriving back at the apartment, Esther went straight to her collection of scrolls. She kept them in a chest next to her couch. The scrolls told the history of Persia. More importantly, they often hid secret notes from Mordecai that had been delivered by Esther's kitchen maid, Mei.

Esther knelt by the chest, lifted the lid, and unrolled the first scroll. She was delighted to see Mordecai's familiar script on a small note. It was written in code as usual, with *one* and *two* meaning Gabe and Izzy.

As always, the note was unsigned. As a further precaution against discovery of her Hebrew background, Esther destroyed the notes after reading them, although it grieved her to do so.

Esther hungrily read the note:

Many maidens have been presented to the king. One and two have new business with the palace. Dina is well again.

She'll marry E. soon. Be strong! Love from all.

Esther's shoulders slumped. A pang of envy swept over her as she thought of Dina marrying. *Oh Lord, forgive me,* she thought. *Make me happy for Dina, not jealous!* She felt alone and hopeless. Her eyes filled with tears.

"Miss! I see you're back. How was your morning?" It was Mei, emerging from the kitchen with a platter of fruit. Esther blotted her tears with a handkerchief.

"What's wrong?" cried Mei. "You're crying black tears!"

"Oh, that's just eye make-up," said Esther. "I got some happy news from Mordecai and it made me cry."

"I'm glad you got pleasant news. Mordecai sent something else for you, but I couldn't hide it in your scrolls."

"Oh?"

"You'll find it under your silks," said Mei with a grin. Esther hurried to her dressing room and opened the jeweled box that held her silks. As she pulled back the soft layers, she was greeted by a small cloth face smiling up at her with purple eyes.

"Basha!" cried Esther, clutching the doll to her chest. "Oh Basha, how wonderful!" she exclaimed. Esther twirled about the room, holding Basha at arm's length, as if giving her a tour of her new home. Mei stood in the doorway, smiling at the happy reunion.

"How about some lunch?" asked Mei. "We have some of your favorites; avocado salad, dates, and soft cheese."

"That sounds perfect," said Esther. "Make some for both of us, and we'll dine in the courtyard. It's a beautiful day!" Mei disappeared into the kitchen.

Esther settled into a chair and sat Basha on her lap, delighting in the doll's familiar face. *How silly,* she thought. *A grown woman making such a fuss over an old doll!* Then she whispered softly, "Mordecai. *Precious* Mordecai! He always understands."

10

A Warning

"I'M AT a loss for words," declared Hegai as he sat admiring Esther. "Who chose the gown?"

"It was Esther's choice," replied Artemis. "She also chose the slippers and the jewelry."

"I must say, Esther," said Hegai, "your taste in fashion is without equal."

"Thank you, Hegai," said Esther. She felt uncomfortable under his gaze.

Hegai struggled to lift his heavy body from the chair. Two servants pulled him to his feet. He approached Esther for closer inspection. "And what is that delightful scent?"

"We mixed it at the perfumery this morning," said Artemis. "It's Esther's creation. Tell me again, Esther, what is it?"

"It's mostly jasmine," explained Esther, "but it has a little sandalwood for relaxation and a touch of violet for sweetness."

"The king will be enchanted!" exclaimed Hegai, rubbing his pudgy hands together.

"Now," he said in a more serious tone, "You will soon be presented to the king and his advisors. There are some important rules to remember. Please have a seat, and listen closely." Artemis and Esther settled carefully onto a couch, smoothing their gowns under them to prevent wrinkles.

"First, always approach the king with your eyes *downcast*," instructed Hegai. "It's a sign of respect. When you are asked to speak, you must hold a silk in front of your lips. It shows you are unworthy to speak to His Majesty with an uncovered face. Do you have a silk?"

"Yes, sir," replied Esther, holding up a lacy silk that matched her gown.

"Lovely!" exclaimed Hegai. "Of course, the king will ask to see your face. In that case, you will lower your silk.

"Second, when speaking to the king, always begin with the words, 'May you live forever.' Or better, 'O king, may you live forever.' Address him as *Your Majesty*. Do you understand?"

"Yes, Hegai," said Esther.

"Next, you must *never* turn your back to the king; always *face* him. If you are dismissed to leave, you must *back* out of the room. I suggest you practice walking backward.

"Finally—and most importantly—you must never speak to the king unless you are *invited* to speak! If you speak without being invited, you will be promptly killed."

"Killed?" gasped Esther.

"Yes! Some have made that mistake and were stabbed to death by the king's guards."

"Oh *no!*" cried Esther. "Have any of the maidens been—"

"Not so far. Don't be the first! Just remember; the king must *extend his scepter* toward you before you may speak to him." Hegai demonstrated by thrusting the top of his cane forward. "If he does this, you are invited to approach the king."

"Does this apply to the queen too?" asked Esther.

"Yes! Now I just want to add that you are in a very select group, my dear. You may have noticed many of the maidens are no longer here."

"I have," said Esther.

"There are good reasons for this. Some have fallen ill and were sent home. Some were caught stealing. Several were too slow to learn. Some flirted with the manservants. Of the remaining maidens, most have been presented to the king, but so far he hasn't chosen anyone. He wants to see them all first. Of those who are left, you are among the very finest."

"Thank you, Hegai," said Esther. "I appreciate everything you've done for me."

"You will do well," predicted Hegai.

11

Three Questions

A FEW DAYS later, Hegai and Artemis appeared at Esther's door. "Are you ready to meet the king?" asked Hegai, his eyes dancing with excitement.

"I'll know after I've met him!" joked Esther, trying to dispel her nervousness. Her servants stood behind her with long faces. Some of them dabbed away tears. They knew Esther would not return to the maidens' quarters. After meeting the king, she would either be sent home, kept as a slave, or become Queen of Persia.

"You look radiant, my dear!" exclaimed Hegai.

"Thank you," said Esther. "Hegai, what about my personal things like my harp and my scrolls?"

"We'll have them sent to you. I promise."

"We must leave now, Esther," said Artemis. "Hegai and I will walk you to the end of the maidens' quarters. The king's servants will escort you the rest of the way. We mustn't keep the king waiting!"

Esther gave her servants a last smile before following Artemis and Hegai into the hallway. Upon reaching the reception hall, they were met by two of the king's escorts. *I may never see Artemis and Hegai again,* thought Esther. She hugged Artemis and thanked Hegai for the harp. *May they know God,* she prayed.

Esther was escorted to the entrance of the king's audience chamber where she waited to be called in. "You look lovely, miss," said one of the escorts. "I'm certain the king will be delighted to meet you."

"Thank you, sir." replied Esther. Frightening thoughts began to plague her. *Will the king be ugly? Will he be cruel? Will he smell horrid? What if I have to marry him?* She drew a deep breath. *Be calm. Remember,* 'I will go with you and make the rough places smooth,' words from the holy books sent in a note from Mordecai.

Suddenly the door swung open revealing a large chamber. The high ceiling was adorned with gold carvings. The walls displayed paintings of Persian kings and princes. Esther saw none of this; her eyes were fixed on the floor, as she had been instructed by Hegai.

King Xerxes was seated on a throne. He wore a tall golden crown and held a scepter. He was flanked by four guards and twenty advisors. Every eye was on Esther. The king extended his scepter to her. She was escorted to the front of the room, a few paces from the king.

"Please tell me your name, miss," said the king.

Holding her silk in front of her lips, Esther answered, "O king, may you live forever! I am your servant Esther."

"I wish to see your face, Esther."

Esther lowered her silk and looked into the face of King Xerxes. She was amazed! He was surprisingly young and handsome! His tanned face was framed by black curly hair and a beard. His dark, shining eyes shone with intelligence and vitality.

The king studied Esther's face for a long moment, then broke into a warm smile. Esther smiled back. She felt her heart pounding. Turning to his advisors, the king said, "You may begin."

Even his voice is handsome! thought Esther.

An advisor stepped forward and addressed Esther. "Miss, each maiden brought before the king must answer the same three questions. You will now be asked these questions. Further questions may be asked as needed."

Lord, give me wisdom! prayed Esther.

"The first question is this," began the advisor. "What are the two most important qualities a queen should possess?"

After pausing a moment, Esther replied, "Sir, I believe a queen should be *kind,* and she should be *wise.*"

"*Kind*, and *wise*," repeated the questioner. The chamber was quiet while everyone reflected on Esther's words.

Then King Xerxes leaned forward and addressed Esther with a challenge. "To *whom* should the queen be kind?"

"O king, may you live forever," said Esther. "The queen should *first* be kind to the *king* because he is her husband. Then she should be kind to the king's *family* and to his *subjects*." Xerxes leaned back, satisfied.

The advisor asked a follow-up question. "Miss, you said a queen should be *wise*. Where would the queen *obtain* this wisdom?"

"Sir, wisdom comes from God," replied Esther.

"Which god?" persisted the questioner.

"Sir, *many* gods are worshipped in the kingdom. I seek wisdom from the God who created the earth. He is an invisible God who—"

"And does this invisible God have a name?"

Esther thought, *If I say the name of God, they'll know I'm Hebrew!* She also knew she couldn't deny her belief. "Sir, the name of the God I worship is—"

"Next question!" interrupted the king. He was growing impatient.

"Miss, the second question is this," said official. "What is the most important job of a queen?"

Esther tried to imagine herself married to the king. "Sir, His Majesty rules over a vast kingdom and has great responsibilities. I believe the queen should serve him by providing a pleasant, relaxing home." Xerxes smiled. He nodded for the next question, his eyes never leaving Esther's face.

"Miss, the final question is this: Should the queen *always* obey the king?"

Remembering what had befallen Queen Vashti, Esther saw a chance to disqualify herself with a truthful answer. "Sir," she said, "the queen should obey the king—*unless* he asks her to do something that would offend *God*." The audience emitted a collective gasp. The other maidens had answered with a simple "Yes."

"Miss, you have insulted the king!" stormed the questioner. The guards drew their swords.

"No, she has not!" thundered Xerxes, rising to his feet. "This maiden speaks the truth! We must *not* offend the gods! A king before me mocked a God and was struck dead that very night!"

Xerxes glared at his advisors. "My father, King Darius, respected the gods. So shall I!" Everyone was still while the king regained his composure.

Then Xerxes did something he hadn't done with the other maidens. He stepped down from his throne and approached Esther. His handsome form was enhanced by a flowing velvet robe. Upon reaching Esther, he lifted her hand and kissed it.

"Thank you, Esther," he said softly. "You are lovely." He paused, studying her eyes. "And you are wise."

"O king, may you live forever! Thank you, Your Majesty," said Esther. It was clear to all that the king was captivated by her.

"The name Esther means *star*, does it not?" asked Xerxes.

"Yes, Your Majesty," said Esther.

"It is a fitting name for you."

12

The Queen

*A*FTER MEETING Esther, the king could think of no one else. He was madly in love with her. He wanted to crown her queen that very day, but he had vowed to meet all the maidens before making his choice.

Esther was taken to another part of the palace to await the king's decision. She was relieved that her worst fears about him had proven untrue. *He's charming!* she thought. *And young! Thank you, God, for your kindness to whoever is chosen.*

As soon as the king had met all the maidens, he sent for Esther. This time, when the doors to the audience chamber opened, the king was standing, flanked by is advisors. Every eye was trained on Esther.

The king extended his scepter. As Esther moved toward him, she knew in her heart what he was about to say. *Oh God, give me strength for what is happening!*

The king strode eagerly to Esther, smiled, and grasped her hand. He whispered for her to lower her silk. Then he stood next to her, facing the audience.

"Gentlemen," he said, "I present Esther, the fairest maiden in the kingdom! It gives me great joy to announce that she shall be your queen!" The audience burst into applause. Esther had won the admiration of all.

The crowning of Queen Esther of Persia was a grand event. It took place in the throne room amid a dazzling array of princes, governors, officials, noblemen and noble ladies from throughout the kingdom. They were dressed in their finest for the occasion.

Esther was radiant in a white gown. A matching cape trailed behind her as she glided the length of the throne room. Flutes and harps played softly. The guests marveled at Esther's grace and beauty.

King Xerxes stood by his throne, beaming at Esther. He wore a purple robe and a fur trimmed cape that hung from his broad shoulders. A magnificent crown gleamed above his handsome face.

When Esther reached the king, the soft music was replaced by a trumpet fanfare. Esther knelt. The king placed a sparkling jeweled crown on her head with the words, "I crown you Esther, Queen of Persia. May you reign forever!"

The king grasped Esther's hand and led her to a second, smaller throne. When they were seated, the audience burst into applause with shouts of "Long live the queen!" Among the officials and nobles in the audience, no one was prouder than Mordecai.

Following the coronation, a great banquet was held. It was called Esther's Banquet, in honor of the new queen. The royal banquet hall was draped in white silk hung from marble columns. Flowers cascaded from elegant urns set on tall pedestals. The marble floor sparkled with inlaid gems—purple, blue, and turquoise. The air was fragrant with perfume.

Guests sat on lavish couches trimmed in gold. They drank from silver goblets. They dined on seafood, wild game, and an endless parade of succulent dishes. Musicians strolled among the guests playing joyful tunes on their lyres and flutes.

Xerxes and Esther greeted their guests while seated on thrones at the head of the banquet hall. Esther was gracious and beautiful. Xerxes was proud of Esther and totally entranced with her.

As guests presented themselves to the royal couple, the king noticed Esther speaking to them in their native tongues. She showed a knowledge of each province. *I have chosen well,* thought Xerxes.

"Haman!" exclaimed the king to a richly dressed man bowing before him. It was the nobleman who vied to spend more time with the king than anyone. "Welcome, my friend," said Xerxes.

"O king may you live forever!" exclaimed Haman. He rose to his feet, his green eyes wide with excitement at being so close to the most powerful man in the world. "Thank you, Your Majesty. May I offer my congratulations to Your

Majesty on the coronation of Her Highness."
He cast a courtly smile to Esther.

"Thank you," replied the Xerxes.

"It has been my honor to faithfully serve
Your Majesty," offered Haman. "I pray to be
of *further* service to you and Her Highness—for
the glory of your *kingdom*, of course."

Haman paused, hoping for encouragement
from the king, but Xerxes looked past him and
extended his scepter to the next guest. Haman
bowed to Esther and moved on. She noticed he
was careful to select the highest-ranking seat
available in the hall.

Returning her attention to Xerxes, Esther
was aware of her growing affection for her
husband. He was kind and courteous, not crude,
as she had feared. He seemed to appreciate her
inner strengths, not just her outer beauty.

Esther felt loved and respected. *God is keeping
his promise,* she thought. *He is "making the rough
places smooth."*

Xerxes spent the first weeks of the marriage
showering Esther with gifts—gowns, jewelry,
flowers, a tiny white kitten, two chatty parrots,

candy, a statue from Egypt, and an opulent new litter for her to ride in. "Is there another gift that would please you, my queen?" he asked.

"O king, may you live forever!" replied Esther. "You have been *so* generous to your servant. However, there is only one thing more that would please me."

"Please tell me, my love. You may have up to *half my kingdom!*" said Xerxes.

"Your Majesty, I desire that my servants from the maidens' quarters be placed in my service here—for they are *dear* to me."

"Your wish will be granted!" declared the king. The next day, when the seven maidservants arrived, there were squeals of joy and tearful hugs for Esther.

Esther had become the joy of Xerxes' life. He spent as much time with her as he could. Every morning they enjoyed breakfast together on their balcony overlooking a flower garden. They talked about the new summer palace they were building in the mountains. On nights when the king fretted about kingdom problems, Esther soothed him to sleep with soft tunes on her harp.

As months passed, wars and uprisings caused Xerxes to be gone for weeks at a time. Esther missed the king, for she had grown to love him. Although her servants were a great comfort to her, she missed her family. When she arranged meetings with Mordecai in the courtyard, he was careful to address her as *Your Highness.*

She would also visit the palace kitchen, not only to help plan the meals, but because Gabe and Izzy made deliveries there. The family shop now supplied the palace with tableware, spices, and wine.

It took every ounce of Esther's will to keep from flinging her arms around Mordecai and her brothers when she saw them, but she continued to obey Mordecai and not reveal her Hebrew identity.

Esther cared deeply about her subjects. She often climbed into her royal litter—minus the trumpeters and banner bearers—and quietly traveled about the city. When she found people in need, she sent food and clothing to them. Queen Esther was greatly admired by her subjects.

13

A Darkening

"YOUR HIGHNESS!"

"What is it?" Esther spun around to see Mei in the doorway.

"It's Mordecai!"

"Mordecai?" cried Esther. "What's happened?"

"He's…he's—"

"Is he ill? Is he…?" Esther couldn't say the word.

"He is not well, Your Highness!"

"Not well?" cried Esther

"He wails and cries in the streets! He's dressed in rags. His skin is gray with ashes, and he cries out. I fear he has lost his mind!"

"Sackcloth and ashes!" cried Esther. "Oh Mei, it means he is grieving! Something terrible has happened! What is he saying?"

"He keeps crying, 'All is lost! All is lost!'"

"Mei, please find my manservant and bring him here at once!"

"Yes, miss." Mei rushed toward the servants' quarters.

Esther fell to her knees, "Oh, Lord, let it not be Gabe or Izzy! I couldn't bear to lose one of them!" *All is lost,* she repeated. *What could it mean?* "Lord," she prayed, "be with Mordecai and comfort him in his distress." Esther was tormented by frightening possibilities.

"Your Highness?" It was Esther's manservant, Hathach, in the doorway.

"Hathach!" Esther ran to him. "I have some urgent business for you. Do you know the king's official, Mordecai the Hebrew?"

"Yes, Your Highness. I have seen him at the palace gate."

"It seems he is in great distress, Hathach. It is a custom of the Hebrews in times of calamity to dress strangely and cry out in the streets. This is not fitting for an official of the king. Please see that he is supplied with proper clothing."

"Yes, Your Highness."

"And please bring me word of what is *troubling* him so that we may offer help."

"Yes, Your Highness."

"And Hathach, see that the king is not bothered with this matter. He is grieving his losses at the hands of the Greeks and wishes not to be disturbed."

"Your servant will guard the king's privacy, Your Highness."

"Thank you, Hathach. Please report to me as soon as you return."

After gathering some clothing for Mordecai, Hathach headed for the palace gate. He found Mordecai wailing loudly, his face streaked with ashes and tears. His sackcloth was in shreds. He was a pitiful sight. "Sir, I have been sent to you by the queen," began Hathach. Mordecai raised his anguished face to the servant, but made no sound.

"Sir," continued Hathach, "The queen expresses concern for your distress. Her Highness wishes to know the cause of your grief so that she may be of help."

Mordecai replied in a tired, raspy voice. "Please thank our lovely queen for her concern.

He found Mordecai wailing loudly, his
face streaked with ashes and tears.

Are you aware that the arrogant Haman was put in charge of the kingdom while the king was away at the war?"

"Yes, sir, and if I may say so, sir, Haman would not have been my choice."

"Nor mine," agreed Mordecai. "Haman was given the king's signet ring so he could issue royal decrees. The first thing he did was require everyone to bow down to him."

"I know, sir."

"I refused."

"You refused? May I ask why, sir?"

"You see, Haman is an Agagite. Our peoples are ancient enemies. Long ago, God commanded us to 'blot out the memory of the Agagite.' When I refused to bow to Haman, he issued a royal decree to have *every* Hebrew *killed*!"

"Has the decree been sent out yet?" asked Esther.

"Yes, Your Highness," answered Hathach, panting from hurrying back with Mordecai's message. "It has been posted in every province and in every language. It calls for all Hebrews to be killed—men, women, young and old, even babies. Their belongings are to be destroyed and their land taken."

Esther collapsed onto a nearby couch, her mind reeling with the news. "When is this great evil to take place?" she asked.

"In the twelfth month, Your Highness."

The twelfth month, thought Esther. *That gives us some time.* "Hathach, please bring Mordecai the Hebrew to me!"

"He cannot enter the palace gate, Your Highness. He refused to change out of his rags."

"Did he accept my offer of help?"

"Yes, Your Highness. Mordecai requests that the queen go before the king and beg His Majesty to save the Hebrews."

"I see," said Esther. "You know I cannot approach the king uninvited. I would be put to death."

"I understand, Your Highness."

"The king has summoned no one lately. He grieves deeply for his losses at the war. Please return to Mordecai and tell him I *dare* not approach the king lest I be executed on the spot."

"Yes, Your Highness."

While awaiting Mordecai's reply, Esther paced nervously about her quarters, trying to devise a way to stop Haman's plan. *I could have him brought before me and threatened with death! No, he has the king's signet ring; he could have* **me** *killed! Perhaps I could arm my servants, have them overpower Haman's guards and—*

Hathach knocked. Esther rushed to let him in. He spoke a carefully memorized message from Mordecai. It carried hard news for Esther. "Your Highness," said Hathach, "Mordecai reminds Your Highness that a *few* of the Hebrews *will* survive, as God has promised." Esther remembered God's promise that the Messiah would come from the Hebrews one day.

"He warns Your Highness," continued Hathach, "that your silence at this time will cause thousands to be killed, including his family."

Esther's shoulders sagged under the weight of Mordecai's answer. *Is there no other way?* she thought. "Did Mordecai offer any advice on how I should approach the king?"

"No, Your Highness, but he did suggest that perhaps the reason you have been made queen is for 'such a time as this.'" Esther pondered the words. *For such a time as this.*

Ever obedient to Mordecai, Esther committed herself to the task. "Please, Hathach, tell Mordecai I will do as he asks. No, wait. I'll write a message." Esther found a piece of parchment and some ink. Using a reed pen, she scratched out a message:

> *I will do as you ask. Have the people cease eating and drinking for three days. Have them pray for me. Then I will approach the king.*
> *If I die, I die.*

Esther knew Mordecai would recognize her handwriting. She rolled up the parchment and handed it to Hathach. "Please keep this out of sight until you deliver it to Mordecai."

14

The Reversal

*F*OR THREE days and nights, Esther and her maids ate and drank nothing. They became weak and parched. They prayed that Esther would receive wisdom and protection. Near the end of the third day, Esther remembered the story of Abigail that her mother had told her many years before. Abigail had overcome evil with good.

The next morning, Esther hurried to the palace kitchen and asked the cooks to prepare a banquet for three. It would include the king's favorite dishes and be served in an opulent room near the palace garden.

Next, Esther returned to her quarters, bathed, had her hair styled, and put on her make-up.

She chose a blue gown, explaining to her maids, "blue means *God's protection*."

"Please pray with me," said Esther. The maids knelt with her, some fighting back tears. "God, I commit this mission to you," Esther prayed. "I know you will go before me and make this rough place smooth, even if I die. Please take care of these precious friends. Amen."

Esther rose and donned her crown. The maids fastened it securely. Then Esther left for the king's quarters.

As Esther reached the king's outer court, she could see him slouched on his throne. He wore no crown. He was alone except for two guards.

Esther softly entered the court and stood where the king could see her. She paused and silently practiced the words she was about to say, knowing they could be her last.

"Queen Esther?" It was Xerxes! Esther turned to see the king extending his scepter to her. She rushed to him and knelt at his feet.

"How wonderful to see you, my queen!" exclaimed Xerxes, struggling to straighten himself on the throne. "Please stand and show me your lovely face." Esther stood and lowered her silk. She was shocked at the king's appearance. He looked older, and very tired. His beard was ragged. His clothes were wrinkled and stained. An empty wine goblet dangled from his hand.

"What is your request, my queen?" said the king. "I will give you up to half my kingdom!"

"O king, may you live forever," said Esther. "If it pleases Your Majesty, I would like you to attend a special banquet this evening. It is for you and your nobleman, Haman. There I will give you my request."

The king smiled for the first time in weeks. The sight of Esther revived him. "We'll be there!" he said. "What time?"

"At sunset," replied Esther. Xerxes rose and dismissed her with a kiss on her hand. Then he sent a message of invitation to Haman.

On returning to his personal quarters, Xerxes relaxed in a long, soothing bath. He had his hair and beard trimmed. He selected a richly decorated robe for the banquet, and had flowers sent to Esther.

Then the king retired to his bedchamber for a nap; he wanted to be at his best for the evening. But sleep wouldn't come, so he ordered his official records brought to him. The records described everything that had happened during his reign.

The king asked his scribe to read the records aloud. At one point, there was an account of a plot to kill Xerxes. It described how Mordecai the Hebrew had overheard the would-be assassins hatching their plan. Mordecai had promptly reported it, thereby saving Xerxes' life.

"Was Mordecai the Hebrew ever rewarded for saving my life?" asked Xerxes.

"I'll see," said the scribe. He scanned the passage. "There is no account of such a reward, Your Majesty."

"Mordecai the Hebrew deserves to be honored!" declared the king.

That evening, Esther was relieved to see her husband looking refreshed as he took the place of honor at her banquet table. *He's still handsome!* thought Esther, choosing to overlook some new battle scars marring his face.

Xerxes was enchanted with Esther. She seemed more beautiful than when he'd first met her.

Haman was in his usual form, showering the queen with compliments and promoting himself to the king. "How lovely you look, Queen Esther!" gushed the Agagite. "Your beauty is unequaled in all the kingdom. Your servant has never tasted such divine food! The pomegranate wine is delicious! And this banquet room is sublime!"

Turning to the king, Haman exclaimed, "Your Majesty's kingdom is unrivaled in all history! Your Majesty's servant is pleased to report that your kingdom has *prospered* under my humble service. I take no credit for myself! No! Rather my success has come from the gods who have bestowed their favor upon me." On and on he babbled throughout the meal.

In truth, Haman and his family alone had prospered in Xerxes' absence. The greedy nobleman had stolen from the king's treasury and set his sons in high positions with extravagant pay.

The king didn't hear most of Haman's blather. He'd been gazing at Esther and absently nodding at Haman now and then, while savoring his favorite dishes.

When the last course was cleared away, Esther and her two guests moved to the sitting area where the desserts would be served. Haman sat on an overstuffed sofa facing the royal couple. Xerxes and Esther sat together, holding hands.

Esther knew the king would soon ask for her request. She was prepared to expose Haman's murderous plan and beg the king to spare her people.

It was at that moment that the king remembered the murder plot against him, and how Mordecai had foiled it and saved his life. "Haman," he said, "Tell me what should be done for a man I want to honor?"

Haman thought to himself, *Who is there that the king would rather honor but me?* So he answered, "For the man the king desires to honor, dress him in a royal robe the king has worn and give him one of the king's horses with the king's insignia on its head. Have this man paraded through the streets on the king's horse!"

Haman's dreams of glory seemed within his grasp. He continued, "Have *heralds* go before this man announcing loudly, 'This is the man the king delights to honor!'"

"Yes!" declared the king, rising to his feet. "This shall be done *at once* for the man I delight to honor—Mordecai the Hebrew!"

Haman was stunned. For once, he was speechless. Esther rose from the sofa and knelt before the king. "O king, may you live forever!" she cried. "How is it that you can so *honor* a man and then have him *killed?*"

"Killed?"

"Yes! Mordecai the Hebrew is to be killed along with every Hebrew in your kingdom—including your *queen!*"

"My queen? How is it that my lovely queen is to be killed?" cried the king.

"Because I am a *Hebrew*, Your Majesty!" Haman's eyes widened in horror. Displaying her bracelet for the king to see, Esther pointed to its inscription. "These words are in *Hebrew*, my king! This was my *mother's* bracelet! I am to be killed along with my people!"

Tears streaking her face, Esther begged, "Please, Your Majesty, save us from this horrible destruction!"

"Who has *dared* to do such an outrageous thing?" stormed the king.

"Your Majesty," said Esther, "the one who issued this cruel decree—and stamped it with *your* ring—" Esther rose and pointed an accusing finger at the cowering Agagite. "—is this vile Haman!"

"B-but, Your Majesty," sputtered Haman. "I can explain, I had no idea—"

"Silence!" thundered the king. "Guards!" Four guards stormed in. "Arrest him!" Xerxes yanked the signet ring from the Haman's hand as the guards dragged the screaming villain from the room. Later, Haman was executed on a high scaffold he'd had built to hang Mordecai.

Mordecai was told the news and summoned to appear before the king. He quickly changed out of his mourning rags, told Gabe and Izzy to spread the news of Haman's death, then rushed to the palace. As he neared the gate, he could hear the sound of rejoicing spreading through the city.

Upon arriving at the palace, Mordecai was escorted into the throne room. There stood King Xerxes with Esther beaming at his side. Xerxes extended his scepter to Mordecai, who walked the length of the hall, his eyes downcast.

He was barely able to contain his impulse to rush up and hug Esther.

"Welcome, Mordecai son of Jair!" began Xerxes.

"O King, may you live forever, thank you," said Mordecai.

"Have you met our lovely queen?"

"Yes I have, Your Majesty." said Mordecai. Esther tried not to grin at this understatement.

"Mordecai," said the king, "I have called you here for two reasons. First, I want to *thank* you for foiling the murder plot against me. I recently became aware that you have never been rewarded for saving my life."

"It was my privilege to serve you, Your Majesty," said Mordecai.

"Second, I want to *apologize* to you and your people for the actions of the wretched Haman. I am afraid I misread his true character. I should *never* have given him charge over my subjects."

"You are most gracious, Your Majesty," said Mordecai. "I will convey your apology to my people."

"Thank you. Now, since Haman's intent was to destroy the Hebrew people, I have seized Haman's considerable riches and given them to our lovely Hebrew queen."

Mordecai and Esther exchanged smiles. At this point, Esther surprised both men. "Your Majesty," she said, "since Mordecai is my *father,* I hereby appoint *him* to manage this great wealth for me."

"Your father?" exclaimed the king. "Mordecai is your *father?*"

"Yes, Your Majesty. Mordecai adopted my brothers and me when we were orphaned. I beg your forgiveness for not revealing this to you, but our people have enemies, as Haman has so cruelly demonstrated."

Xerxes pondered this news for a moment as he studied Mordecai's noble face. Then the king began pacing in front of his throne while stroking his beard. He thought, *So this is the man who saved my life, and raised my queen to be so lovely and wise!*

Finally, the king spoke. "This is what will be done for Mordecai the Hebrew, the man I desire to honor for saving my life: He will be dressed in royal robes. A crown will be placed upon his head." Mordecai's eyes widened in disbelief. "He will ride my steed through the streets and be praised by all my subjects!"

"Mordecai son of Jair," continued the king, "will write a *new* decree that will stop this terrible threat against my queen's people. He will seal the new decree with my ring." Xerxes pulled the signet ring from his own hand and placed it on Mordecai's middle finger. Esther's eyes brimmed with tears of joy.

"Finally," concluded Xerxes, placing his hands on Mordecai's shoulders, "the man I honor will be *second only to me* in my kingdom! All of this will be done because Mordecai son of Jair, is loyal, and courageous, and deserving of honor!"

Mordecai stayed at the palace that night. Esther was overjoyed to be under the same roof with him again. She pampered him with a beautiful guest room, delicious food, and soft sleeping clothes. They stayed up late into the night, chatting about all that had happened.

"Mordecai, isn't it *strange* how you and Haman have switched places?" said Esther.

"What do you mean *switched places*?"

"I mean, he was once in charge, and now you're in charge. He was wealthy when you were in sackcloth. Now you're wealthy and he's lost everything—including his *life*."

"I know, daughter. I think it shows that, no matter how bad things look, we have to do the right thing, and trust God. He has a way of using evil for good."

The next day, Mordecai donned a royal robe and crown. He rode on the king's stallion, led by royal heralds. He carried the new decree that stopped Haman's wicked plan. Grateful crowds cheered as Mordecai the Hebrew rode through the city.

Later that day, as Gabe was displaying a copy of the new decree in the shop window, Esther's litter stopped in front of the entrance and was immediately engulfed in a throng of admirers.

Esther emerged from the litter wearing a soft green gown. She strode quickly into the shop and locked the door to keep the crowd away. "Gabe!" she said.

Gabe wasn't sure how to react to his royal sister, but managed an awkward "Ma'am!" Esther hugged Gabe and whispered, "Is Izzy here?" Gabe grinned and nodded toward the back room. Esther tiptoed to the doorway. She saw Izzy unpacking a crate of dishes.

"I hope those beautiful plates are for the palace!" she said. Izzy froze at the sound of Esther's voice. He looked up to see his sister smiling at him.

"Esther! Is it really you—here, in the shop?"

"Of course it's me!" cried Esther, "I'm still your sister!" She rushed to Izzy and hugged him. Gabe joined in. "I've missed you both so much!"

"You've saved us all!" exclaimed Gabe.

"How could I *not?*" said Esther. "You two mean everything to me! Besides, it wasn't *me*. It was *God. He* made a way. I'll tell you all about it at dinner."

"Dinner?" said Izzy.

"Yes, I'm here with a royal invitation. The king wants to meet both of you!" The brothers gaped at Esther in disbelief. "He wants you to come to the palace tonight to celebrate the new decree. Mordecai will be there too."

"But the Sabbath starts tonight," said Gabe.

"I know," said Esther. "And the palace is more than a Sabbath's walk away, so you'll have

Esther tiptoed to the doorway.
She saw Izzy unpacking a crate of dishes.

to stay the night. We can spend the day together! It's been ages since I've had a real Sabbath."

"What can we bring?" asked Izzy.

"Just bring yourselves," said Esther. "Oh, one more thing; we could use more of that pomegranate wine we've been buying from you. The king loves it."

"No problem," said Gabe. "We just got some in. You know what we say—"

"I haven't forgotten," said Esther with a grin. "If you don't have it, you can't sell it!'"

The Hebrews throughout the kingdom of Persia held a great celebration. Feasting and dancing went on for weeks. To this day, in the spring of the year, the Hebrew people set aside a day to celebrate their deliverance from destruction. The day is called *Purim*. It celebrates Queen Esther of Persia, the Hebrew woman who believed God, and accepted His calling for her life.

Be strong and courageous.

Do not be afraid..of them, for the
Lord your God goes with you;
He will never leave you or forsake you.

Deuteronomy 31:6

The Celebration of Purim

*E*STHER'S BRAVERY in saving her people is still celebrated by Hebrews around the world during the month of March. The holiday is called Purim, a word that means *freedom from evil*. It's a festive occasion that includes singing and dancing, listening to the Esther story, exchanging gifts, and giving gifts to the poor.

Celebrants often dress as characters from the Esther story, and act it out. Whenever the villain Haman is mentioned in the skit, the audience reacts with foot stomping and old-fashioned noise-makers called *groggers*.

A popular Purim treat is *Haman Taschen* or "Haman's Pockets," triangular cookies filled with poppy seeds, fruit, chocolate, or peanut butter.

Acknowledgements

*J*ANE CLARK, Janet Day, Cindy Gatten, Mary Gunderson, and Joan Hamilton for excellent help with the manuscript.

John Gunderson for encouragement and patience.

God for his many blessings.

Copies of *Jewel of Canaan* and *Star of Persia* by Marion Dawson Gunderson are available at:

www.amazon.com
www.barnesandnoble.com
bookstore.westbowpress.com

To learn more about the author and the Brave Beauty Series, visit
www.BraveBeautyBooks.com."

Printed in the United States
By Bookmasters